The Secret Mermaid

Seahorse SOS

Sue Mongredien

Illustrated by Maria Pearson

For Hannah Powell with lots of love

First published in the UK in 2010 by Usborne Publishing Ltd., Usborne House,
83-85 Saffron Hill, London EC1N 8RT, England. www.usborne.com

A CIP catalogue record for this book is available from the British Library.

FMAMJJASOND/10 96093

ISBN 9781409506324

Printed in Reading, Berkshire, UK.

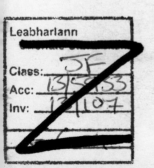

Contents

The **Mermaids** of the

Shanti

Molly

Eloise

Leila

Undersea Kingdom

Queen Luna

Aisha

Iona

Phoebe

Chapter One

"Home time!" called Mrs. Cartwright. "See you next week, everyone!"

It was a Friday afternoon in mid-November and, as the children rushed out of the classrooms, it seemed as if everyone was talking at once, about birthday parties, weekend shopping trips, sleepovers... *Everyone except me, that is,* thought Molly Holmes, trudging along on her own, as the voices rang out around her.

Molly had been a pupil at Horseshoe Bay Primary School for just two months. Back in the summer, she and her family had moved from their old town to live with Gran in Horseshoe Bay, and it had been really scary starting a new school without knowing anybody there. Molly still missed her old friends, especially Katie, and didn't feel as if she quite fitted in here yet, especially as the other girls in her class already had best friends, or were in tight-knit groups. And a few of them lived in the same street and walked home together in a gang, whereas Molly's new home was further out of the village, up on the cliffs overlooking the bay.

Still, I wouldn't swap that *for anything,* Molly thought, her spirits rising as she headed towards the cliff path. She loved living by the sea, especially since she'd discovered some of the ocean's magical secrets. *And I may*

not have lots of school friends yet, she said to herself, *but at least I've got my mermaid friends...*

A pale sun was struggling to shine, and the beach was deserted. The sea was grey and choppy, with big rough waves splashing against the rocks – it seemed a totally different place from the summer, when the sand had been crammed with holidaymakers: sunbathing, playing beach cricket, collecting shells and making sandcastles.

Molly didn't mind. In fact, she rather liked the wide emptiness of the beach now; there was something special about seeing it in late autumn, when everyone else had gone. She glanced at her watch – it was three-thirty. There was still plenty of time before it got dark, so she decided to climb down the steep steps to the sand and walk home along the beach. It was too cold to even *think* about paddling, but there was always something interesting to see in the bay, even at this time of year.

The sand was damp, and her school shoes left footprints as she walked along. A strong breeze gusted in from the sea, and Molly felt herself brightening. The school week had finished, and she was on the beach, and maybe, just maybe, she'd get to see her mermaid friends again soon. She never felt happier than when she was diving through the water with them, having wonderful underwater adventures.

Molly's gran had started it all off when she'd given Molly a special shell pendant the day they'd moved in with her. That very night, Molly had discovered that the shell had magical powers,

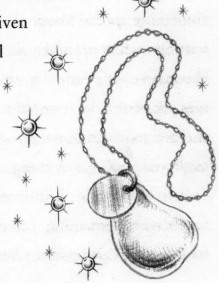

which turned her into a mermaid and took her into the Undersea Kingdom. As the new "secret mermaid", Molly had had all sorts of extraordinary adventures. She had met the Shell-Keeper mermaids and helped to defeat the wicked Dark Queen Carlotta, a bad mermaid who had tried to seize control over the oceans. Since the Dark Queen had been banished, the Undersea Kingdom had been a much happier place and Molly had enjoyed getting to know all the other friendly mermaids and sea creatures who lived there. The only slightly frustrating thing was, she never could tell when the shell's magic would work, and she hadn't had a mermaid adventure for a while now...

Lost in thought, Molly only just managed to dart out of the way when a foamy wave crashed near her feet with a splash. She ran further up the sand, laughing, and started to pick her way over some black shiny rocks, wondering what the tide had left behind today. She'd become good at spotting the different kinds of creatures in the seaweed-fringed pools – small fish called blennies, usually, but sometimes there would be a sea scorpion, or even a shanny – a funny little fish that changed colour to match its surroundings.

She put her school bag down and squatted by the largest pool for a look. There were several strands of sea lace waving in the water – long, thin cords of olive-green seaweed – and some crimson seaweed that Molly knew was called sea oak. The water rippled in the breeze, then a movement from the other side of the pool caught Molly's eye.

A large brown crab with white markings on its back seemed to be pinned under a heavy stone. Its front pincers were scrabbling at the sand as it tried to get free, but it was quite stuck. "Don't worry," Molly said to the crab. "I'll help you."

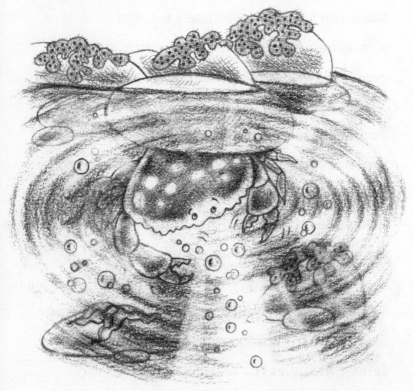

She rolled up her sleeve, leaned over the pool and plunged her hand into the icy water to heave up the edge of the stone. The crab scuttled sideways at once and vanished into the sandy base of the pool. Molly was just about to let the stone drop again when she saw something sparkling beneath it.

Curious, Molly pulled the stone higher and peered down into the pool. How strange! She wasn't sure *what* the sparkly object was down there. It was round and clear, and about the size of a cricket ball. It looked rather like a large, watery bubble...but the way that its surface glittered a faint gold made it seem almost magical.

Heart thumping, Molly tugged the stone right away so as to fully uncover the sparkling ball-thing. Then she reached into the water with both hands, but the ball was slippery and difficult to pick up. *It's like trying to hold a lump of very wobbly jelly*, she thought, as it fell from her grasp for the third time.

By cupping the ball in her hand, Molly finally managed to lift it to the surface of the water for a better look. What *was* it? She had absolutely no idea. Some kind of unusual sea creature which had been washed up far from its usual home? She'd never seen anything like it in her seaside spotter books though, or when she'd been exploring the oceans with the mermaids. Molly was about to take the ball right out of the pool, but then she realized if it *were* a living thing, like a rare kind of sea anemone, that might not be a good idea – she didn't want to harm it.

"Weird," she said under her breath, running a finger over the surface of the watery ball. It felt cool and rubbery, and…oh! What was that moving inside?

Without letting go of the ball, she shuffled onto her knees and then onto her belly, so that she could lean even further over the water for a closer look. The rocks around the pool were wet and cold, even through her coat, but Molly didn't care as she peered into the ball.

There seemed to be thousands of tiny *things* drifting around inside it, as if they were alive. They seemed distorted, the way the world did when you looked at it through the bottom of a drinking glass, but there was something about the shape of the moving specks that was vaguely familiar... They reminded her of something, some creature, but she couldn't quite put her finger on what.

The sun came out suddenly, making the ball glitter brightly in Molly's hands, with thousands of twinkling lights sparkling from it. *It really does look magical*, she thought in wonder. In fact, she had the strong feeling that there was something very special about this peculiar ball...

Before she could think anything else, though, the water in the pool churned as if it were being stirred up very fast by an invisible

hand, and the sudden movement made Molly
jump. "Oh!" she cried in surprise, jerking
back, and dropping the ball. A mist of sand
whirled up in the pool and the ball was lost
from view.

Molly sat back on her heels, eyeing the
pool warily. What was going on? It couldn't
have been a gust of wind that churned up
the water so fiercely – the
breeze had
dropped away
to nothing.
She shivered,
feeling cold,
and rubbed
her hands
together
to warm
them up.

By now, the water was becoming calm and clear once more. The sand was settling back to the bottom and she could see that the strange jelly-like bubble-thing had rolled down into a crevice almost out of sight.

"Weird," she muttered, picking her way gingerly down from the rocks, and glancing back at the pool. She would have to ask her mermaid friends about it next time she saw them, to see if they had any ideas.

The thought cheered her up and she made her way hurriedly home.

Chapter Two

Up at the house, Molly's mum had got a wood
fire roaring in the old stone fireplace of the
living room, and Molly stood before it
thankfully, warming her numb toes and hands.

"Look at the state of your coat," her mum
said, shaking her head at the wet, sandy
splodges over its front as she hung it over a
chair to dry. "Have you been rolling around on
the beach or something, Molls?"

"Sorry, Mum," Molly said. "I went to look in the rock pools."

Her mum's eyes narrowed but she was smiling. "Hmmm," she said. "Crawling all over them too, I reckon."

Gran, who was sitting in her favourite armchair, had a twinkle in her eye. "Her father was just the same, you know. He'd be out in all weathers, having great fun getting soaking wet and covered in sand. It's the magic lure of the beach, that's what it is."

Molly's mum laughed. "Is that right?" she said. "Well, I'd better make you a hot drink, Molly. Magic lure or no magic lure, I don't want you getting a chill."

She bustled into the kitchen, scooping up Molly's baby brother Toby on the way. Toby had just learned to crawl and had been having a lovely time pulling out all the CDs from their rack and bashing them together.

Molly was left in the room with Gran and turned to her, eager to see if she could shed any light on the afternoon's strange happenings. "Gran, I found this really odd thing in a rock pool just now," she said. "It was a sort of ball-thing, about this big –" she spread her hands apart – "and it felt like jelly. Sparkly jelly. Have you ever seen anything like that before?"

Gran looked baffled. "No, I can't say I have," she said. Her brow furrowed as she thought. "And it definitely wasn't a jellyfish?"

Molly shook her head. "No, it was round. Could it have been some kind of…egg? Or a weird creature? Something really rare?"

"I don't know what it could have been," Gran said after a moment. "Maybe a toy that had been washed up by the tide? Or a dog's ball, even? There were lots of dog-walkers out today."

Molly shrugged. "Maybe," she said, although she wasn't convinced. The ball-thing had seemed too unusual, too pretty, too *magic* to be just a toy or a dog's ball, but she didn't want to say that, with Mum only a few metres away in the kitchen. She gazed out of the window at the beach and saw that the tide was coming in now, creeping up the sand.

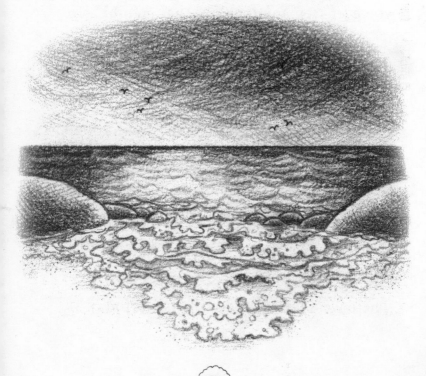

Soon the sea would have covered all the rock pools and the strange ball might be pulled back out into the ocean… But what was it? she wondered again. And hadn't it been strange, the way the water had swirled around all on its own in the pool?

Gran leaned forward now, her eyes more serious than Molly had ever seen them. "Promise me something, Molly," she said in a low voice. "Promise me you'll take extra care down on the beach for a while. Just in case…"

Her voice trailed away as Mrs. Holmes came in at that moment with steaming mugs of hot chocolate for everyone. Molly was more intrigued than ever, though. What had Gran been about to say? Did *she* think there might be something magical about the ball Molly had found? It wouldn't surprise her.

After all, many years ago, when Gran had been a girl, she had been the secret mermaid herself, and had had her own adventures under the sea. She of all people knew that the ocean had some wonderful, mysterious secrets that most humans never got to hear about or see.

Molly's mind raced with thoughts, as the beach gradually fell into darkness and evening drew in. She hoped more than ever that she'd visit her mermaid friends that night!

As Molly got undressed for bed later on, she made sure that her special shell necklace was nearby on her bedside table. The shell itself was part of a magical conch and, although it looked ordinary enough, it was the powers of the conch which took Molly into the mermaid world to become the secret mermaid. Threaded onto the chain next to the shell was a silvery charm, which Molly had been given by a kindly walrus after the Dark Queen had been banished. The charm shone different colours, depending on the way you held it, and sometimes Molly thought she'd seen animal shapes appearing on it. The walrus had told her it was a gift from the many sea creatures she'd helped on her last adventure – and that if she was ever in trouble in the ocean, one of them would come to her rescue.

Thankfully, Molly hadn't yet needed to use it, but she was sure it would come in handy one day. Besides which, it looked beautiful, glinting against the pale, curving piece of conch shell on the necklace.

She said goodnight to her parents and gran, then got under the covers quickly, shivering – partly with the cold, but partly with excitement. The more she thought about it, the more convinced she was that the thing in the rock pool really had been magical.

She rolled over in bed, trying to get comfortable…and noticed that the shell on her necklace was gleaming in the darkness, shining a pink pearly light. A thrill rushed through her at the sight. The mermaid magic was beginning!

Molly shut her eyes immediately, and then, a single heartbeat later, felt as if she were falling from a great height, plummeting incredibly fast. A tingling spread all over her, and her legs felt as if they were dissolving… Then came the rushing sound of water in her ears, and she opened her eyes.

Hurrah! A shimmering green tail swung where her

legs had been before, and she was back in the
Undersea Kingdom. And there was
the kindly Merqueen herself,
swimming to greet her,
a smile on her wise,
beautiful face.

Molly bobbed a curtsy, still in awe of the majestic Queen Luna. "Hello," she said shyly.

Queen Luna gave Molly a hug. "It's good to see you, secret mermaid," she said. "But I'm afraid we need your help again." She drew apart from Molly and her smile gave way to a grave expression. "Something terrible has happened in the oceans!"

Chapter Three

Molly gulped. That sounded serious. Before she
could reply, though, the queen turned and
beckoned to a group of mermaids who were
swimming towards them. Molly didn't recognize
them and looked around, feeling confused. It
was only then that she noticed the huge pink
scallop shell nearby, surrounded by large
smooth rocks with fronds of emerald-green
seaweed rippling gently behind them, and she

realized where she was – in the courtyard garden of the queen's palace. She'd been brought here by her mermaid friend Ella, the very first time she'd become a mermaid and met the Merqueen. A prickle of anticipation ran down Molly's back as she wondered why she'd been brought here again. Surely Carlotta, the Dark Queen, hadn't returned?

"Ah, you're here," Queen Luna said to the new arrivals, ushering them to sit on the large rocks,

which were covered in soft sea moss. She settled herself in the pink scallop shell, before making introductions. "Molly, I want you to meet our Animal-Keeper mermaids – Aisha, Eloise, Phoebe, Iona, Leila and Shanti. All of you, this is Molly, our secret mermaid. She helped us greatly with the banishment of Carlotta."

Molly said hello to the Animal-Keeper mermaids, who smiled at her in return.

"Hey," said Aisha, the mermaid with a glossy black bob, staring at Molly's necklace. "Is that what I think it is – the animal charm?"

Molly looked down. "Yes," she said. "A walrus gave it to me. He said if I ever needed help, the ocean creatures would look after me while I was wearing it."

"Cool!" said Eloise, who had blonde bunches and wide blue eyes. "You must have done something amazing to be given that.

Those charms are really rare." She grinned at Molly, her eyes twinkling. "I wish I had one!"

Molly smiled back, liking friendly Eloise instantly. "Your necklace is nice too," she said politely, seeing the silver seahorse pendant that swung from the chain around Eloise's neck. "Oh – you've all got them," she realized, seeing the diving dolphin symbol on Aisha's necklace, and various other animal images on the others' chains.

"That's right," smiled Iona, who had a long brown ponytail, violet eyes and a scattering of freckles. "We all look after certain animals in the ocean, and these charms help us do that." Her soft eyes became unhappy. "Although they're not much use now, unfortunately."

"Why?" Molly asked. "What's happened?"

The Merqueen gave a sigh. "We have a big problem," she said. "Certain types of animals have completely disappeared."

Molly didn't understand. "What do you mean?"

"They've gone," Eloise said sadly. "I have searched and searched in all their favourite places but I haven't seen a single seahorse. And yes, they're very good at camouflaging themselves, my seahorses, but they can't actually turn invisible. I just don't know where they can be."

"The penguins have gone too," put in Phoebe, who had pink sea-flowers woven through her brown hair. "Not even a feather to be seen. They love playing tricks on me, but I know this isn't a trick. This is serious."

"Even the whales have vanished," said the mermaid called Leila, her pretty heart-shaped face clouded with worry. "They've disappeared, every last one of them. I thought they must be hiding at first, but..." She shrugged.  "Where do you hide a blue whale? They're just not there any more."

Molly was alarmed by this news. She'd made friends with many different sea creatures since she'd begun her mermaid adventures, and particularly loved the gentle whales, especially the kindly humpbacks who'd helped her and Delphi, one of the Shell-Keeper mermaids, in the past. "So...are *all* the animals missing?" she asked. Then she frowned, as a thought struck her.

"No, they can't be. I was on the beach just this afternoon and saw a crab in one of the pools."

"That's the peculiar thing," red-haired Shanti said. "The turtles have all disappeared, but other shelled creatures, like crabs and lobsters are fine."

"And the squid are still out there, but the octopuses have gone," Iona put in. "It's a mystery."

"A mystery we can't solve," the Merqueen agreed. "We've tried looking into the Seeing Stone and asking it for the creatures' whereabouts, but nothing comes up." She patted the large white rock nearby with a sigh. "I'm worried there is some bad magic afoot, the way these particular animals have vanished overnight."

There was a silence for a moment while Molly tried to take everything in. "So which animals have gone?" she asked.

"The whales, the penguins, the turtles, the seahorses, the dolphins and octopuses," the Merqueen said, counting them off on her fingers. "Our Animal-Keeper mermaids look after one species each, protecting and caring for their different animals. But nothing like this has ever happened before. Have you heard or seen anything strange in your world that might explain their disappearance?"

Molly shook her head. "No," she said. "But..." She remembered the unusual bubble-like ball she'd found in the rock pool, with the floating specks. The tiny specks, as small as

commas on a page, had reminded her of
something and she suddenly realized what.
Seahorses!

"'But'?" prompted the Merqueen, leaning
forward. "But what? Do you have any clue,
any information at all that might help with
our search?"

"Well, it's probably nothing," Molly said,
feeling silly for even thinking about it, "but I
found something weird on the beach today, in
one of the rock pools..."

She described how she'd found the peculiar
sparkly ball, and how the
water had suddenly
churned up in the
pool. She shrugged
at the end of the
story, not quite able
to meet the Merqueen

in the eye in case the wise monarch was looking disbelieving. "They were only tiny, but there were *things* moving inside the ball. Living things, I'm sure. Now I think about it again, they were like thousands of miniature seahorses, but..." She felt herself blush. "But obviously they were too small. Unless the ball I saw was some kind of egg?"

Eloise looked up with interest, her eyes bright. "I'm the mermaid who looks after the seahorses," she said. "But it can't have been a *seahorse* egg. The babies grow in a pouch inside the father seahorse who gives birth to them." She twirled one of her bunches around her fingers thoughtfully. "I'm curious, though. Would you be able to show me where you saw this ball?"

"Of course," said Molly, relieved that Eloise hadn't just dismissed her story as nonsense.

"Although now that the tide is up, it might not be there any more…"

"Well, let's look, anyway," Eloise said, her shimmering blue tail flicking from side to side. "The sooner the better!"

Molly nodded, feeling excited at the thought of another adventure.

The Merqueen's face was solemn. "Do take care," she warned. "If there is bad magic involved, you must be on your guard. However, you have your piece of the conch, Molly, and Eloise has her seahorse pendant, both of which can work great magic – as can Molly's animal charm. Together, you should be well-protected."

Molly nodded. "Okay," she said, and turned to Eloise. "Let's go."

Chapter Four

With the other mermaids wishing them good
luck, Molly and Eloise left the mermaid palace
and swam out of the Undersea Kingdom in
the direction of Horseshoe Bay. Mermaid
swimming was effortless compared to
swimming as a girl, and Molly surged through
the water at great speed, her hair streaming
behind her, and the rocks and seaweed
blurring below.

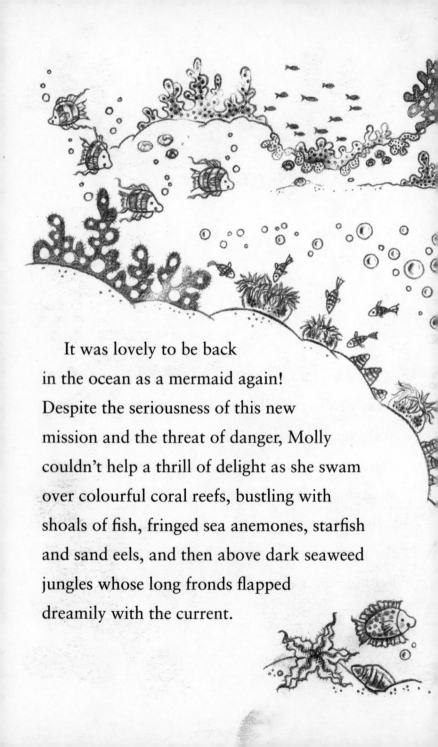

It was lovely to be back
in the ocean as a mermaid again!
Despite the seriousness of this new
mission and the threat of danger, Molly
couldn't help a thrill of delight as she swam
over colourful coral reefs, bustling with
shoals of fish, fringed sea anemones, starfish
and sand eels, and then above dark seaweed
jungles whose long fronds flapped
dreamily with the current.

It was a long way to Horseshoe Bay and Molly's feelings of happiness gradually gave way to worries and doubt. What if she'd got it all wrong about the ball? What if it really was just a dog's toy, as Gran had suggested? She'd feel such an idiot. On the other hand, what if the ball *did* have something to do with the missing seahorses, and Molly and Eloise were swimming into some kind of trap?

The whole thing was very unsettling, Molly thought, as she followed Eloise's sleek form through the deep blue water. Whole species didn't just go missing overnight. They must have been taken away by someone or something. But where? And how?

"I didn't know seahorses could camouflage themselves," she said, remembering something Eloise had said earlier. "How do they do that?"

"They're amazing," Eloise said proudly.

"They change colours according to their backgrounds, so that predators don't see them in the seagrass or coral. Very cool!"

"That is cool," Molly said. "I wish I could do that." *I'd blend right in to my classroom wall so nobody would notice I didn't have any friends,* she thought with a pang.

"Ah, here we are," Eloise said just then, and took Molly's hand, steering them into the bay. "So...show me exactly where you saw the ball."

Molly stared around, trying to get her bearings. She had been to the bay as a mermaid before, when she'd helped her friend Ella find her piece of the magic shell, and it felt like a totally different place from when she came here as a human. It was night-time, but with her special mermaid eyes, Molly could see perfectly well in dark water, and everything appeared light under the surface of the sea.

She gazed about, and spotted a familiar-looking cluster of rocks. She was pretty sure they were the ones in which she'd been searching earlier that day. But the tide was high now and the rocks were deep below the water. Surely the strange sparkly ball would have been washed away?

"Let's look over here," she said to Eloise. "I think this is where I was rock-pooling."

Molly led the way to the rocks, trying to remember where she'd found the ball. Then she spotted the brown crab she'd rescued, which had such distinctive white markings on its shell. It was in a large, bowl-shaped section of the rock and Molly felt sure that this was the very pool where the ball had been.

She held her breath, hoping the ball would still be there, but at the same time dreading that it would turn out to be completely unmagical. She would have wasted Eloise's time and she'd have made a fool of herself. Worst of all, they'd be no nearer finding the lost seahorses – or any of the other missing animals.

Her heart pounded uneasily, but just then a golden gleam caught her eye and she darted to the far side of the rock to investigate. Yes – there it was. She picked it up for a closer look, peering at the specks inside, which were still darting and flurrying like living creatures. Her pulse quickened as she put one eye to the ball to get a better look. The creatures *did* look like seahorses!

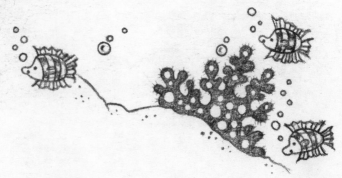

"Here!" she called to Eloise excitedly. The ball was still glittering brightly without any light shining onto it, so surely it must be magical, she thought to herself, hope rising within her.

Eloise's eyes widened when she saw the ball –
and what was inside it. "Oh my goodness," she
said in a hushed voice. "That's them – that's my
seahorses!" She clapped a hand over her mouth
in shock. "But they're so tiny. How—?"

She broke off, looking alarmed, and glanced
around anxiously. "I don't know how this has
happened," she said, her voice trembling. "But I
do know this – that bad magic must have caused
it. Very bad magic indeed!"

Chapter Five

Molly felt a chill run through her. Thank goodness she'd decided to walk the long way home from school and explore the rock pools! If she hadn't, the poor seahorses might have been stuck in their watery prison for ever. "We need to get them out," she said. "And we need to turn them back to their usual size. Somehow…" Her voice trailed away. She didn't have any good ideas about how to do either of those things.

Eloise was nodding, deep in thought. "Yes," she said, "we must set them free as soon as possible. Look at them all crammed in together! And what if there's no food in there? They could be starving." She scooped up the bubble and pressed it cautiously.

"Maybe we can burst it somehow, if we squeeze hard enough. Mind you, I would hate to injure any of the seahorses. What if one of them got squashed?"

"Can we use our magic to open it up?" Molly suggested. She held her piece of conch tightly. "Conch, please set the seahorses free!" she begged.

Her shell glowed a soft
pink but nothing
happened, and
Molly's shoulders
slumped in
disappointment.
She knew her
piece of the magic
conch shell was
capable of amazing
feats, but she still wasn't
entirely sure how to harness its powers.

Eloise grabbed her seahorse pendant and
pressed it against the bubble, muttering a string
of magical-sounding words. Still nothing
happened. She prodded the ball again. Its
rubbery surface moved but didn't burst.
"There must be some way we can break it,"
she muttered, squashing it between her palms.

The miniature seahorses swirled around inside the ball when she did so, but remained trapped.

Just then, a movement caught Molly's eye. Scuttling over to them with its peculiar sideways walk was the brown crab, its stalky eyes wiggling. "Hello there!" it cried in a scratchy sort of voice. "Don't I recognize you from somewhere?"

Molly smiled. "You do – but I look a bit different," she said. "I was the girl who helped you get free from under that stone earlier. Only I'm a mermaid now!"

"So you are," the crab said. "Never forget a face, me. And what luck that I can thank you for your kind action!"

He bowed his two front pincers low in front of her, then raised them again. Then he did a jerky little side-to-side dance in excitement, pointing a pincer at Molly's necklace. "Oh, I say!" he spluttered. "Is that...is that an animal charm you're wearing?"

Molly nodded. "Yes," she said, smiling at the awestruck look on its face.

"Oh my goodness!" the crab said, unable to keep its legs still. "Then you really are a friend – a friend to every animal." He bowed even lower. "And I am at your service, my dear. For now and ever more!"

"Thank you," Molly replied, not sure what else to say. She almost wanted to laugh at the crab's earnest expression, but managed to hold it back. She didn't want to offend him.

"Yes, all the ocean's creatures are at your beck and call while you have that charm, you know," the crab went on. "If ever you need assistance or—" He broke off and stared in surprise at Eloise, who was trying to bite into the sparkly ball. "What *is* she doing?" the crab asked Molly in a low voice. "Is she quite all right?"

Molly told the crab about the missing seahorses and he listened in dismay. "My word, that's terrible," he said, sounding indignant.

"Terrible! Who could have done such a thing?" Then he clicked his front pincers together and wiggled his eyes. "Would you like me to have a go? These pincers are much sharper than teeth, you know."

"Yes please!" Eloise replied, overhearing.

The mermaids held the ball while the friendly crab pressed the end of his pincers against it.

However, despite trying repeatedly, he was unable to pierce it. Finally he lowered his pincers, looking gloomy. "Sorry, my dears," he said. "If only I were a bit bigger. Perhaps we could look for a lobster – one of them might oblige. Or—"

"*Or*," Molly interrupted, an idea popping into her mind, "we could try using some mermaid magic to make *you* bigger. What do you think, Eloise?"

Eloise nodded, her face lighting up. "That might work. Would you mind?" she asked the crab politely.

The crab danced on the spot. "Mind? Not at all! Be my guest!" he cried.

Eloise held tightly to her seahorse pendant and muttered a magical command. Molly clutched the animal charm on her necklace too, just in case it helped.

A flurry of electric-blue sparkles shot from
Eloise's pendant and swirled around the crab...
and all of a sudden, he was huge! His body was
about the size of a cocker spaniel,
with enormous long pincers
that he stretched in front
of him with glee.

"I say! Look at me! Look at ME!" he cheered excitedly. "Goodness, I'm quite gigantic. Isn't it wonderful? Now, pass me that ball, my dears. I'm sure these whoppers will make quick work of bursting it!"

Molly and Eloise carried the ball to him and he took it between his mighty pincers. "Please be careful," Eloise begged him. "The seahorses will be very fragile now that they're so small, and—"

But she never finished her sentence. For below them, the seabed was rippling and shuddering, and a mist of sand had blown up around them, making it very hard to see.

"What's happening?" Molly shouted in fear.

"I don't know!" Eloise called back. "Hold on, I'll use my pendant to shine a light..."

Molly's hands flailed in front of her as the water grew murkier and muddier. Sand stung her eyes and she blinked. Now she couldn't see anything! And then, all of a sudden, she felt something cold and scratchy grabbing her around her waist, and sharp claws digging into her skin.

"Help!" she screamed.

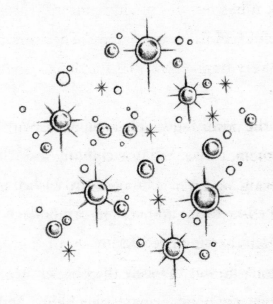

Chapter Six

"Get off!" Molly squealed, wriggling away from the scraping claws. What was *that*? And what did it want with her? Oh, how she wished she could be like the seahorses and camouflage herself so it couldn't see her!

Just as she was thinking this she felt her animal charm bounce against her skin...and a prickling sensation spread through her body. A second later, a bright light shone through the gloom – and Molly could see Eloise holding her shining pendant as if it were a torch. Both mermaids cried out as they saw a sandy-brown creature lunging towards Molly before recoiling

from the light. Molly stared, her heart thudding in fright. The creature had a vaguely human-shaped head, and long muddy arms that ended in claws. It was half-buried in the sand,

as if it had burst up from the seabed.

Eloise shone the light straight at the creature and it collapsed, sinking down into the sand and disappearing from sight. The sand mist settled, and Molly realized that Eloise was staring at her in shock.

"How did you do *that*?" she asked.

"Do what?" Molly replied, puzzled.

"Vanish like that," Eloise said.

"Vanish?" Molly echoed. What was Eloise talking about?

Eloise rubbed her eyes and stared at Molly again. "It was very strange," she said wonderingly. "When that creature grabbed at you, you just…disappeared. And now you're coming back again…how peculiar!"

Molly felt completely confused. What did Eloise mean? She hadn't disappeared. She'd been here the whole time! Then she glanced down at herself and gasped. Her tail was completely black, like the rocks behind her, whereas her top half was a pale, glimmering version of the way she usually looked. As she

watched, her body
gradually brightened
and returned to its
normal colours, with her
tail reappearing last of all.

"How did that happen?" she
breathed. Something magical had taken place,
but Molly didn't have a clue what, or how.
But then again... Her mind raced, as a thought
occurred to her. She'd made a wish about

wanting to camouflage herself like seahorses did
so that the scary creature couldn't see her, hadn't
she? Had that wish somehow come true?

Before she could think about it any more,
a cry of triumph went up from the crab. "I've
done it! Look!"

Molly and Eloise swung round to see the
crab waving a pincer in delight. He'd managed
to puncture the sparkly ball and was now
carefully tearing a larger hole in its surface.

Molly swam over, just as a stream of clear
water gushed out of the ball...and then out
poured thousands of miniature seahorses! As
they swam out, the seahorses grew bigger and
bigger until they were back to their usual size.
Some of them seemed a little dazed, but most
bobbed around chattering happily to one
another, some turning joyful somersaults in
the water.

Eloise hugged about ten different seahorses, looking happy and relieved. "I'm so glad to see you all. Are any of you hurt? And how did you become trapped in there in the first place?" she asked.

"We…" started one beautiful golden seahorse with tiny spines down his back. Then a confused look appeared in his eyes.

"I don't know," he said. "I can't remember."

"Nor me," a brown seahorse said. "One minute I was out in the reef, and then..." He shook his head. "And now I'm here. What happened?"

Silence fell and Eloise bit her lip. "Does anyone remember?" she asked. "Something must have captured you all, shrunk you to a tiny size and then trapped you in a bubble. Surely one of you can tell me what happened?"

The seahorses stared at one another blankly. "In a *bubble*?" one echoed in disbelief.

"What are you talking about?"

"Shrunk to a tiny size?" another said, gazing down at himself in bewilderment. "I look the same as ever. Don't I?"

"What are we doing here, anyway?" a small red seahorse asked. "This isn't our home. How did we get here?"

Eloise's face fell. "They don't remember anything," she whispered to Molly in dismay. "They're confused. This is horrible!"

Chapter Seven

Molly felt worried too. Seahorses were usually busy, alert little creatures who knew everything that was going on, but now they seemed bewildered and blank. "At least we found them," she said, trying to be positive. "And they're safe."

Eloise glanced around. "Yes, for now," she said shakily. "But I don't want to take any chances, not after that monster-creature we just saw." She raised her voice and spoke to the seahorses.

"Okay, guys, I'm going to send you back to your proper homes now where the water will be warmer," she said. "I'll come round and check up on you all properly later." She clutched her pendant, which glittered between her fingers. "Off you go!"

The seahorse pendant shone brightly for a moment, then a rush of blue-tinged bubbles appeared, whisking the seahorses away in a fast-moving stream. "Wheeeee!" they cheered excitedly. "Thank you!"

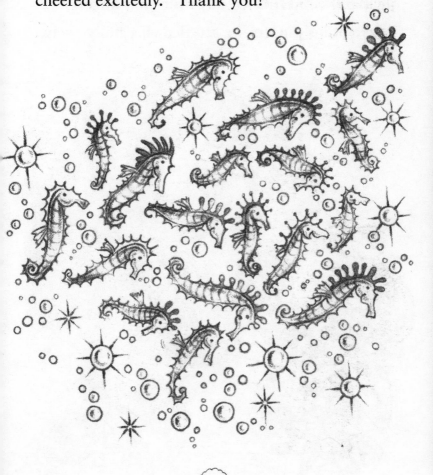

Next, Eloise used her magic to return the crab to its normal size. She and Molly thanked him for all he had done.

The crab looked rather bashful. "Happy to help," he told them. "Any time!" And with a wave of his pincers, he scuttled cheerfully away.

Molly and Eloise swam a safe distance away from the rocks, then Eloise stopped and pointed ahead. A silvery light was falling through the water, and Eloise turned to Molly. "Does that mean it's time for you to go?"

Molly nodded. Each of her mermaid adventures ended at sunrise – which always arrived too soon for Molly. "I'm glad we found the seahorses," she said, hugging Eloise. "But what do you think that creature was?"

Eloise's smiled slipped away. "I don't know," she confessed. "I've never seen anything like it – and never want to again. I'm going to go straight to the Merqueen now and I'll tell her what we saw – maybe she'll know what it is."

"Do you think it trapped the seahorses?" Molly asked, aware that she didn't have long left in the mermaid world. Her mind was full of questions about what had happened, and she couldn't bear the thought of leaving without getting some answers.

Eloise screwed up her mouth uncertainly. "I don't know that either," she replied. "Whatever caught the seahorses used some very powerful magic to shrink and imprison them like that. And as for that sandy creature... Well, it was so scary, the way it went for you like that. Was it guarding the seahorses, perhaps?"

"I wonder if—" Molly began, but she never got to finish her sentence. A whirl of bubbles spun up around her, and she just had time to call out goodbye before she felt herself being pulled, very fast, away from Eloise and up towards the surface.

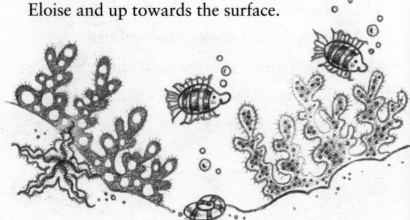

Molly woke up, feeling groggy. Her mind swam with strange images from her dreams…sand-monsters and seahorses…a giant crab…a sparkling bubble…

She sat up in bed, suddenly feeling more alert. No – it hadn't been a dream. All those things really had happened! A shiver ran through her as she remembered the feel of the sand-monster's cold clawed hand on her skin. She didn't like the thought of that creature being anywhere near Horseshoe Bay. What was it doing there? And what did it want?

She picked up her necklace, which had returned to her bedside table, and looked at her animal charm thoughtfully, turning it between her fingers. As the morning sunlight fell upon its silvery surface, a hologram appeared suddenly –

of a beautiful seahorse, like a
tiny wingless dragon, with
its knobbly spined back
and its blunt little
nose. She stared at it,
thinking about all the
seahorses she and
Eloise had set free with
the help of the friendly crab.
Were they safe from harm now, or were they
still under threat? And had they remembered
anything about what had captured them yet?

Molly clambered out of bed and went to
look out of the window, shivering in her
pyjamas as she gazed down at the rolling grey
sea. Somewhere out there were the other missing
creatures – the whales, dolphins, penguins,
octopuses and turtles. She hoped she'd be able
to help the mermaids find them too.

The Animal-Keeper mermaids' faces danced into her mind – Eloise, of course, and Aisha, Leila, Phoebe, Shanti and Iona. Then she found herself thinking about Carlotta, the evil Dark Queen who had enslaved so many sea creatures before, when she had tried to take control of the ocean. Maybe she had something to do with this new mystery...

Molly wrapped her arms around herself, fearful at the thought. But even though she was scared at the idea of facing Carlotta again, she knew she would do anything to help her mermaid friends. And she also knew that she'd be in for another exciting adventure the next time she became the secret mermaid...

The End

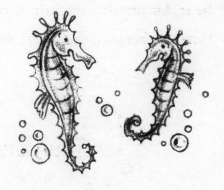

Read on for a sneak preview of Molly's next magical underwater adventure...

Dolphin Danger

Molly was tucked up in bed, feeling cosy and warm as the storm raged on outside her window. Rain was still lashing against the glass and she pulled the covers up higher around her ears, drowsily thinking about dolphins. Then she caught sight of a familiar soft pink light from her bedside table and her heart quickened – her magic shell was glowing! She closed her eyes, and in the very next moment she felt as if she were falling down, down, down. The special magic was working…she was being called to the mermaid world!

Seconds later, she sensed warm water against her skin and opened her eyes, a delicious feeling of excitement spreading through her. Yes! She was a mermaid again, down in the ocean with her very own beautiful green tail sparkling below her, and her shell necklace around her neck. A lobster scuttled by on the seabed, turning stalky eyes towards her with interest, before vanishing in a clump of swaying emerald seaweed. Pretty white scallop shells gleamed where they lay on the golden sand.

Molly happily flipped her tail fin to and fro and was sent somersaulting through the water, with bubbles swirling all around her.

Being a mermaid was such fun!

"Hey! Molly! Is that you?" came a shout, and Molly looked around to see a dark-haired mermaid swimming towards her.

Molly waved in recognition. "Hello!" she called.

Last time she'd been here in the Undersea Kingdom, Molly had met all six of the special Animal-Keeper mermaids who protected various species of ocean creatures. The mermaid in front of her now was called Aisha. Molly thought she looked very striking with her shiny black bobbed hair, cut in a sharp fringe. Her eyes were deep brown and almond-shaped, and she wore a bright pink top patterned with small pieces of orange shell.

The Animal-Keeper mermaids looked after one type of animal each, and the six mermaids

Molly had met looked after seahorses, dolphins, penguins, whales, turtles and octopuses. Aisha was the dolphin mermaid, Molly remembered, spotting the silver dolphin charm that hung around Aisha's neck.

"It's wonderful to see you," said Molly eagerly. "How are you?"

Aisha gave a friendly smile. "I'm good, thanks," she replied. "Eloise told us how you two rescued the seahorses together – good stuff! You did a great job!" Then her face fell. "I still haven't found my dolphins though, and I've been searching everywhere for two days now. I'm starting to worry something terrible has happened to them."

Molly bit her lip. "Has there been no sign of them at all?" she asked.

Aisha shook her head. "Not a thing," she said. "I got really excited earlier when I met a group of seals – they said they'd thought they'd heard some dolphin noises in this part of the ocean. Very very faint, they said. I was so relieved and happy I rushed straight here…but I've searched all over this area now and still haven't found a thing, let alone thousands of dolphins! The seals must have got muddled up, bless them. I'm sure they were only trying to help but…" She shrugged. "I'm so disappointed!"

Molly gave her a hug. Poor Aisha did look miserable. "Maybe we could go together to a different part of the ocean and—" she began, but then broke off, and listened hard. Was that a tiny clicking noise she had just heard? She strained her ears and caught the faint sound of high-pitched whistling. "Wait," she gasped. "I'm sure I just heard something. Listen!"

To find out what happens next, read

To find out more
about Molly and all her
mermaid friends, and have
some magical ocean fun,
check out
www.thesecretmermaid.co.uk

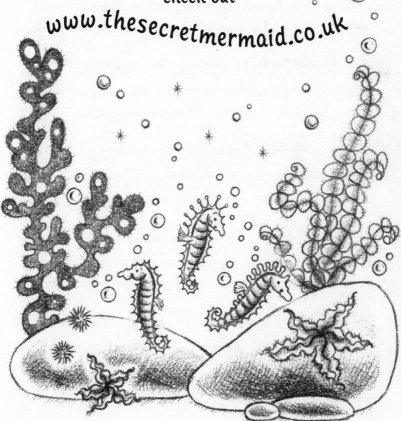

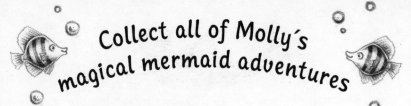

Collect all of Molly's magical mermaid adventures

Enchanted Shell ◎ 9780746096154

Molly is transported to the Undersea Kingdom for the first time, where she discovers she is the secret mermaid!

Seaside Adventure ◎ 9780746096161

To help Ella recover her piece of the magical conch, Molly must find a way to trap an angry killer whale.

Underwater Magic ◎ 9780746096178

Can Molly find some pirate treasure to win back Delphi's shell from a grumpy sea urchin?

Reef Rescue ◎ 9780746096192

Molly must help Coral find her shell to restore the ocean reefs, but a swarm of jellyfish stands in their way…

Deep Trouble ◎ 9780746096185

Pearl's conch piece is trapped in an undersea volcano and guarded by sea snakes. How can she and Molly release it?

Return of the Dark Queen ◎ 9780746096208

Molly must save Shivana from an Arctic prison before the Shell-Keeper mermaids can finally face the Dark Queen and complete the magical conch.

Seahorse SOS 9781409506324

There's more trouble in the Undersea Kingdom and Molly joins in the search for the missing seahorses.

Dolphin Danger 9781409506331

Molly and Aisha can hear faint calls for help but the dolphins are nowhere to be seen. Where can they be?

Penguin Peril 9781409506348

Could the Dark Queen be behind the mysterious disappearance of the penguins from the icy seas?

Turtle Trouble 9781409506355

There are some scary monsters lurking in the coral reef and they're guarding the turtles Molly has come to set free!

Whale Rescue 9781409506393

Molly must not only save the trapped whales but also her mermaid friend, Leila.

The Dark Queen's Revenge 9781409506409

The Dark Queen is back and she wants to rule the Undersea Kingdom with her bad magic. Can Molly put an end to her vile plans?